Hi! I'm Eddie.
Eddie Carlson.

This is a story about me
and my three best friends
– Haggis, Fiend and Norman.
They're monsters.

That's right. **Monsters**. Big hairy
critters with fangs and horns
and extra eyes.

They were living in the basement of
the house my family moved into.
Don't tell anyone, will you?
They're a secret. Only me, my parents
and my big sister Angela
know about them.
And it isn't easy keeping
it that way . . .

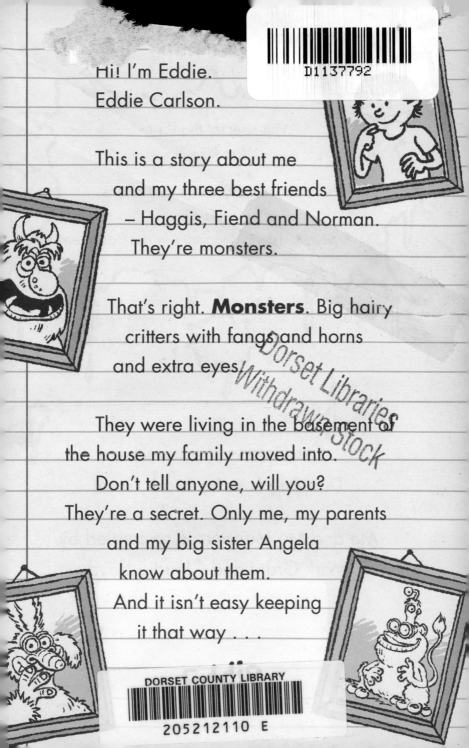

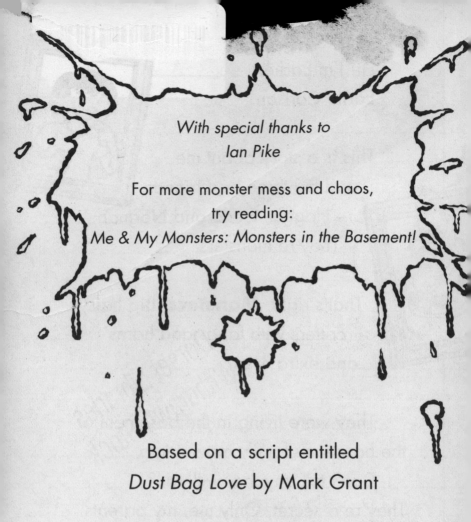

With special thanks to
Ian Pike

For more monster mess and chaos,
try reading:
Me & My Monsters: Monsters in the Basement!

Based on a script entitled
Dust Bag Love by Mark Grant

Me and My Monsters is co-created by
Mark Grant and Claudia Lloyd

Me & My MONSTERS™

Monster Mess

RORY GROWLER

PUFFIN

PUFFIN BOOKS

Published by the Penguin Group
Penguin Books Ltd, 80 Strand, London WC2R 0RL, England
Penguin Group (USA) Inc., 375 Hudson Street, New York, New York 10014, USA
Penguin Group (Canada), 90 Eglinton Avenue East,
Suite 700, Toronto, Ontario, Canada M4P 2Y3
(a division of Pearson Penguin Canada Inc.)
Penguin Ireland, 25 St Stephen's Green, Dublin 2, Ireland
(a division of Penguin Books Ltd)
Penguin Group (Australia), 250 Camberwell Road, Camberwell, Victoria 3124, Australia
(a division of Pearson Australia Group Pty Ltd)
Penguin Books India Pvt Ltd, 11 Community Centre,
Panchsheel Park, New Delhi – 110 017, India
Penguin Group (NZ), 67 Apollo Drive, Rosedale, Auckland 0632, New Zealand
(a division of Pearson New Zealand Ltd)
Penguin Books (South Africa) (Pty) Ltd, 24 Sturdee Avenue,
Rosebank, Johannesburg 2196, South Africa

Penguin Books Ltd, Registered Offices: 80 Strand, London WC2R 0RL, England

puffinbooks.com

First published 2011
001 – 10 9 8 7 6 5 4 3 2 1

Copyright © Tiger Aspect Productions/The Jim Henson Company/Sticky Pictures Pty Ltd 2011
Me & My Monsters ™ & © Tiger Aspect Productions/The Jim Henson Company/
Sticky Pictures Pty Ltd 2011
Me & My Monsters is produced by Tiger Aspect Productions, The Jim Henson Company
and Sticky Pictures Pty Ltd
All rights reserved

Set in Futura Standard
Printed in Great Britain by Clays Ltd, St Ives plc

British Library Cataloguing in Publication Data
A CIP catalogue record for this book is available from the British Library

ISBN: 978–0–141–33668–8

www.greenpenguin.co.uk

What a Mess!

BANG!

'Eddie!' **CRASH!**

'The house is a mess! Look at this place!'

People say the most fearsome creature known to man is a lion. Not true. An angry mum is far more deadly. She can kill you with just one look. If you come across one in the wild, my advice is to play dead.

'*EDDIE!*'

Mine had her teeth bared, ready to pounce.

'I know you're alive, Eddie. I can see you breathing.'

Sometimes even the best plans don't

work. I stood up from the floor, where I had been doing my best to lie still under a rug.

'And there is no point in trying to hide from me, Haggis,'

Mum carried on. 'especially not behind a hatstand.'

'I'm not here,' said Haggis, trying to breathe in and make himself thin enough not to be seen behind something one hundredth the size of him.

'Where are you then?' Mum was right in front of him now, but he still wouldn't give up. Like me, he knew when to keep out of her way.

'I'm somewhere else,' rumbled Haggis.

Mum looked round the room. 'Are you *all* somewhere else?'

'Technically, I was never here,' called out Fiend.

Mum's eyes narrowed like a shark

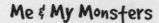

on the prowl in the water and she spotted the rest of her prey in seconds. Fiend was hiding in a plant pot and Norman had a lampshade on his head in the hope that, if he couldn't see anyone, it meant that nobody could see him.

Mum sighed. 'Right, Edward. Listen and listen carefully. This is really important.'

Serious stuff: she only ever called me Edward when I was in massive trouble or when she wanted to get a point across. I made sure to listen carefully.

'Maria from the cleaning agency
will be here any moment to deal with
all this mess. And as I'm late and
have got meetings all over town, I'm
asking, begging, that you *please* keep
the monsters in the basement until she
leaves. Do you think you can do that?'

'Of course I can,' I said,
just as a massive cloud
of noxious gas blasted
through the room,
picking up everything
in its path. Haggis
had finally come out
of hiding.

'And you said
this house couldn't
get any more stinky,'

9

I grinned. 'I win.'

Mum gave me one of those looks that said this was not the time for jokes.

'Please don't eat me,' I begged, whimpering.

'What's the point in having children if I can't **eat** them?' She grinned. It was a thing we always did. Mum would pretend to eat me and I would pretend to be scared. Maybe I was getting a bit old for it, but then again, right now, I was a little scared. She really did look cross.

I sighed; it was time to do as we were told.

'Come on, guys, you heard the lady. Back to the basement.'

'I'd wait a bit if I was you,'

said Fiend, dusting a bit of mud off
his fur. 'Haggis might have made a
teeny-weeny little smell down there.
It should be clear by the middle of
next week.'

'**Warfle!**' agreed Norman.

The monsters really weren't
doing anything to help the situation.
I sometimes wondered if they ever
knew just how close they came to
being chucked out on a daily basis.
Still, somehow they always seemed to
manage to find a way round Mum and
Dad and survive.

Just then, my sister Angela marched
into the room. Have you ever noticed
your sister marching around the house?
It happens quite a lot here.

'I'm on half-term break, which is
good,' said Angela. 'But I have nothing
to do, which is *bad*.' She flopped
down on a chair grumpily.

'Come on, you've got buckets of
friends.' Dad was doing his best to
cheer her up, but I could see he was
going to have his work cut out.

'Yeah, back in Australia.'

'Well, surely you've made *some*
friends here?' You had to give Dad
credit; he didn't give up easily.

Angela sighed deeply and stared
sadly out of the window.

'Put it this way, I only ever get text
messages from two people and one of
them is Mum.'

Dad laughed. 'Do you want *me*

to text you?'

'Did you hear that thud?' she said, angrily picking at the sofa.

'No,' said Dad.

'It was the sound of my life officially hitting **rock bottom**.'

'I had a rock bottom once,' said Fiend. 'There was this stone and –'

'Yes, thank you,' I interrupted. 'But we really need to be going downstairs now.'

I grabbed a packet of chocolate-chip cookies and started laying the trail. I had been planning

on scoffing the lot myself later, but
desperate times called for desperate
measures. Anyway, it was
working. Norman was already
heading my way and the others would
soon pick up the scent.

'Just make sure nobody disturbs
Maria!' shouted Mum, as we retreated
towards the basement. 'If I have to
live in this mess one more minute, I'll
explode!'

Dust

'You can't keep us locked up in our five-star, luxury basement!'

It wasn't going well. The monsters were doing everything they could to give the impression of three prisoners serving a life sentence in jail. Haggis, was carving notches in the wall to mark how many days he had been held. I wanted to point out that it was more like three minutes than eighteen years, but at least he was out of trouble and out of Mum's way for the moment. Norman, on the other hand, was sadly blowing into a mouth organ and sighing deeply, as if he had forgotten

what the outside world
looked like. I tried to reason
with them.

'Mum says you have
to keep away from the
cleaner,' I pleaded.

'What is a cleaner anyway?' asked Fiend.

'A cleaner is a person who comes to the house and tidies up,' I said,  trying my best to waft away the smell, previously left by Haggis.

'People do that?' said Fiend, looking puzzled. 'But what's the point?' He really was confused. 'It'll only get messed up again. It always does. You can't fight *nature*.'

'I know that, but try telling my parents. They're obsessed with keeping the house tidy.' And they were too.

Especially when it came to me leaving
stuff on my bedroom floor. Honestly,
anyone would think my dirty socks
were going to explode or something.

'*Pap, theek, flonk,*' said Norman.

'He wants to know what the cleaner
does with all the rubbish,' Fiend
translated.

'Bags it up and takes it away,'
I answered. Helpfully, I thought, but
Fiend was horrified at the suggestion.

'She steals our dirt?'

he cried.

'We must
STOP her!'
rumbled Haggis.

'**IMMEDIATELY!**' agreed Fiend.
He grabbed an old umbrella, tucked
it under his arm like an army general
and began marching towards the
door. Haggis jumped into step behind

him: they looked like a furry army on manoeuvres, heading for the Western Front. Or in this case, up the stairs of our basement.

'**YOU CAN'T!**' I said, trying to get in their way. 'I promised Mum I'd make sure you stayed down here.'

'Monsters have rights, too, you know!' Fiend cried.

'And they have lefts,' mumbled Haggis helpfully.

I held up a hand to shush them. Not just because once Fiend got going there was no stopping him, but also because I'd noticed something was **missing**.

'Where's Norman?'

He was nowhere to be seen and,

even more worrying, there was a noise coming from upstairs. A noise that sent shivers down my spine. The sound – of a vacuum cleaner!

Love at First Sight

I crept to the door of the kitchen and opened it. There was a lady in a uniform who I guessed must be Maria from the cleaning agency. She was already working away, sweeping the floor. As I watched, I felt a furry presence or two at my shoulder. The monsters were good at creeping up on you. Quite often, the first thing you notice is a bit of a tickle on your cheek or in the case of Haggis, a blast of warm air against your leg.

'Put the broom down and step away from the grime!' cried Colonel Fiend. He was ready to pounce, but I managed to grab hold of him just in time.

'Will you be quiet?' I hissed. 'If she sees you, we're done for.'

'But that dirt belongs to us!' Fiend was really taking this to heart. The situation was getting dangerously out of control. Mum had asked me to keep the monsters in the basement but they were already roaming free, and trying to stop Maria from cleaning.

On the plus side, though, we had found Norman. I could see him on the other side of the room, singing quietly, with an odd smile on his face.

'**Doo doo doo doo doo doo doo doo. Doo doo**,' he murmured softly.

'What's he doing?' I muttered. 'Maria might see him any second!'

'He's **flirting** with the vacuum cleaner,' whispered Fiend.

'The last time I saw Norman act like this, it was with a rubbish bin. Nice-looking, terrible breath. She had it all.'

It would only be a matter of seconds before Maria spotted him. I decided it was time to act. I grabbed the power cord and slowly pulled the vacuum cleaner towards me. It worked. Norman followed it closely, a strange look in his eyes.

'Beep, grrrwww, waaa.'

'Come on, Norman. Just a few steps more . . .'

The vacuum cleaner slid along slowly towards us. Then suddenly – disaster struck. It stopped. The cord

must have got snagged somewhere.
I yanked at it, but it still wouldn't budge.

I began to panic. Norman was
shuffling forward to grab it and it could
only be a matter of time before Maria
caught sight of him. I tried again to
shift the vacuum cleaner and luckily,
this time, it started moving again. I
breathed a huge sigh of relief. It was all
going to be OK. A few more short steps
and I'd have Norman out of there and,
with the aid of the chocolate-chip
cookies, I should be able to get
all of the monsters
back to the basement.

'Weep, bah, brachet, doog.'

Something was happening I
really hadn't banked on.

27

It was like that with the monsters. You could imagine every possibility in your head, but then something you could *never* imagine would happen right at the last minute. In this case, it was Norman thinking his new love was getting away from him. Having found her so soon, seeing her disappear slowly out of sight was breaking his heart, and he started to squeak pitifully. The sort of noise you or I might make, having just been given the world's **biggest, gooiest, chocolatiest ice cream**, to then have it snatched away.

Maria heard the sad squeaks and looked up. While we're on the subject of noises, there is one that my Mum makes when she's stressed. It's usually after I've been chasing one of the monsters around the kitchen and we accidentally land in the dinner she's just spent hours making. Well, a sound very similar to that was now coming out of Maria's mouth.

'ARGH! EEEE!'

29

I ran in quickly.

'What is *that*?' shrieked Maria, pointing at Norman.

'Please don't worry. It's just, er, a toy.'

I know Norman's not a toy, but it was all I could think of and I really didn't think the truth would help right now.

'His eyes are following me,' she said, moving from side to side.

'It's, er, remote control . . . look.' I picked up Dad's calculator and started frantically pushing buttons in Norman's direction.

'What kind of family would have something like that, eh? It's, oh, it's grotesque! What is it? A reject?'

Fiend came storming out, clearly upset by her comments. Monsters can take things very personally sometimes.

'Aaaaagggghh!'

There was that noise again from Maria as soon as she spotted Fiend. '**There are more!**'

'Yes, yes, there are.' I tried to convince her. 'I've got lots of toys, you see.'

'Yeah. I'm this year's *must have*,' announced Fiend, posing. He strutted about for a second or two, like a model on the catwalk at a Paris fashion show, rather than a monster who's just upset the one person in the world my mum wanted us to stay away from.

'**AAAARGGHH!** It speaks!' Maria staggered backwards away from him.

I tried to act calmly in the hope that she would think this kind of thing was just a normal, everyday occurrence.

'Oh, you're not kidding. It never stops talking. I sometimes think I should *take his batteries out.*' I glared at Fiend.

'Aaaaagggggghh!'

Maria was off again. I felt sorry for her, really I did, but this constant yelling was giving me a headache. Haggis had wandered in, causing the latest round of shrieking.

'Hello. I'm . . . stupid.'

This was clearly the final straw for Maria. Did you know that there

is a certain slow way a cupboard
falls when you push it too far? I found
this out after Fiend got his tail stuck
underneath a cupboard in the living
room, and I was helpfully trying to get
it free. Well, if you know that certain
slow fall, that was how Maria went
down: a clean faint. A bit like the time
Angela passed out when Fiend jumped
out of her sock drawer to scare her.

I looked down at our
unconscious cleaner.
'This is so **not** good.'

It Was All a Bad Dream

'Is she dead?' Fiend was poking her.

'I hope not,' I muttered. 'Mum will be furious.' I grabbed his arm, trying to stop him from jabbing Maria too hard.

'Would one less cleaner be such a bad thing?'

'Fiend, that's an **awful** thing to say!'

'Well, someone's got to stand up for all the dirt.' Fiend was now leaning over her.

'Wakey-wakey, dead cleaner thingy person,' joined in Haggis. 'Hokey, pokey, pokey.'

I saw that Maria was starting to stir.

'Quick, get yourselves hidden.' I told the monsters. 'If she sees you again, we're done for.'

I bundled them all quickly behind the sofa. I'm not really sure why I bothered. Especially when it came to

Haggis. It was quite obvious where he was hiding because his bottom was sticking up over the top of the sofa. Still, at least it wasn't facing Maria as she came round. I mean, I know I've had some surprises in my time, but that would be just too much for anyone. It seemed pretty clear to me that Maria wasn't terribly good at dealing with shock. Especially judging by the noise she was currently making.

'Nnngghhhh!'

I leaned over her. 'Are you all

right? You seem to have fainted.'
**'Monsters, boggly eyes, fur . . .
a tail,'** she murmured. They were

EVERYWHERE!'

I pretended to look confused.
Something I have become good at
since the monsters had burst into my
life. It's like when they're trashing Dad's
garage and even though I know it will
end up with me getting into trouble, I
can't stop them because I'm laughing
so much. And then when Dad finds
out what happened, I have to pretend
I know nothing about it, there's a face
I always try pulling – as if to say,
'Garage? What garage?' I had that

face on now with Maria.

'Monsters? What monsters?' I said, acting confused.

'There was one just there.' She pointed. 'And then his eyes . . . and you tried to say . . . toys. Not toys. **Monsters**.'

I shook my head, worried. 'I think perhaps you need a lie-down. Your imagination's running away with you.'

Maria sat up slowly. 'Maybe a lie-down would be a good idea. Will you tell your mother I wasn't feeling well?'

'Oh, don't you worry about her. I'm pretty much the boss around here. I mean, she likes to give the impression she's in charge, but it's all down to me really. You go home and have a nice cup of tea.'

As she started to walk towards the door, I made sure I was always between her and the sofa. Haggis's bottom was waggling about in the air and it wasn't the best view, especially to someone like Maria who was clearly feeling a bit nervous.

She stopped suddenly and looked back to where Norman had been standing, dancing slowly with the vacuum cleaner.

'Definitely no monsters?'

I shook my head sympathetically and steered her out as if helping an old lady across the street. As we reached the door, Angela appeared, bored and looking for friends. She held out her hand to Maria.

'I'm the new girl. Let's get together sometime, yeah? See a movie. Call me!'

Maria looked at her sadly. **'Monsters?'** She wandered out and we heard the door slam. Angela sighed.

'Great. Still nobody to hang out with apart from three furballs and my brother. Could life get any **worse?**'

Actually, it could. We'd managed to lose Maria and now Norman was running away with the vacuum cleaner.

An Angry Mother
Never Sleeps

'**Ding!**' Norman said lovingly, cuddling the handle of the vacuum cleaner.

'Don't they make a perfect couple?' said Fiend.

'Gadgets love Norm,' said Haggis.

'Mm. He's got the movie-star looks and she's got her plastic in all the right places. A real tutti-frutti.' Fiend was now wiping away a tear, so moved was he by the picture of love before us.

Norman leaned on a button and the vacuum cleaner purred into life, sucking up chocolates from a discarded tray from the mess on the living room floor. Haggis was impressed. 'She sure likes her chocolate. That is one sweet-toothed lady.'

'I'll say,' agreed Fiend. 'Mind you, it's not often you see a girl eat the wrappers, too.'

I tried to get my head round the fact that we'd managed to drive the cleaning lady away. I was desperately trying to work out a plan B when Haggis and Fiend started humming. They do that sometimes – any excuse for a song.

'Bom bom bom bom,' started Haggis.

'She hoovered up his heart, Now they'll never be apart. It's a groovy dust bag kind of love,' Fiend crooned.

'*A dust bag love, oh oh oh oh oooohhh yeeeaaahhh.*' Haggis was really giving it his all now. He reminded me of my Aunty Maureen at Christmas. Mind you, her voice could shatter glass.

'*He has a thing for dirt, Let's hope he don't get hurt,*' crooned Fiend.

'Beep boo beerrr.' Norman wasn't really paying attention – too busy nuzzling the vacuum cleaner nozzle.

'A groovy dust bag kind of love,
A groovy dust bag kind of love,
Bah doo bee doo doo,

Hoooo oooo WWveeerrrer...'

Really quite beautiful if you like that kind of thing. I, on the other hand, had more important things to worry about. Mum had just walked in the front door and I could tell that she was far from happy. I think the main clue was the amount of steam coming out of her ears. Does *your* mum do that when she's cross?

'I've just had a phone call from Maria. It seems our cleaner is now our ex-cleaner.'

I was all set to explain everything, but I could tell from the look in Mum's eyes that now was not a good time to interrupt her.

'She was nearly **hysterical** and kept muttering . . . something about

toys and monsters. Toys and monsters
. . . over and over again.'

'I tried to keep them in the basement.
Honestly I did.' I took a deep breath,
finally managing to get a quick word
in. 'I'd have needed an all-you-can-eat
bogey buffet to keep them occupied!'

'It took me so long to find her.'
Mum sank into a chair, head in her
hands. 'Now we'll never be free of this
mess. **Ever!**'

'I'm really sorry, Mum.'

'I don't blame you, Eddie . . .' she
said turning to look at the monsters.
'I blame . . .

THEM!'

Fiend, Haggis and Norman had no idea how much trouble they were in. They were standing together, smiling happily, Norman still cuddling the vacuum cleaner. Honestly, if you didn't know them better, you would think they were all quite cute and completely innocent. It's quite a gift. I wish I had it.

'Heeellooooooooo!'

said Haggis, noticing he was being watched. Mum rose to her feet.

'Right, that does it. I'm sick and tired of cleaning up after you and I'm not going to do it any more.'

'That's **GREAT** news!' Fiend didn't seem in the slightest bit worried. In fact, some might say he looked more than a little bit pleased.

'Yeah, it's for the best,' agreed Haggis.

Anyone would think they had missed the point completely. I, on the other hand, was fully up to speed with the situation. Mum was basically saying she was really very, very fed up with them.

'So, **congratulations**,' she carried on. 'You got the job.'

That stopped them short.

'What job?' asked Fiend blankly.

'The *cleaning* job,'

Mum answered.

'I don't remember applying for the position,' said Fiend, looking at Mum as if she wasn't very bright. 'I did once try to apply for the post of Queen of England, but Eddie here said I couldn't because I wasn't a woman, a human being or in line to the throne. How picky can you get?'

'All three of you monsters applied for the cleaning job when you scared Maria away,' said Mum firmly.

'**OOH! I got a job!**' said Haggis, bouncing up and down. Fiend shook his head and rolled his eyes. All nine of them.

'I expect the kitchen and the sitting room to be *spotless* by the time I get back.' Mum strode towards them with purpose.

'NO, NO, NO, NOOOOOOOO!'

said Fiend. He was standing his ground. 'We're *monsters*, see? We *make* the mess.' 'We don't *clear up* the mess. There must be some mistake.'

That's the thing with Fiend. He never thinks he's done anything wrong, he never bothers being scared when he's in trouble. I wish I could learn to do that.

'Yeah,' joined in Haggis. 'You've got the **wrong** furry guys!'

'If you've got a room that's too *tidy*,

give us a call,' explained Fiend. 'We can give it that "lived in" look in next to no time. It's kind of our speciality.'

'Pah!' cried Mum. 'Anyone can *make* a mess!'

Uh-oh. I could see the warning signs. Mum was about to go mad.

Fiend laughed, completely unaware. 'Oh, no. No, no, no. Not like *we* can.'

'Want to bet?' said Mum and then, taking even me completely by surprise, she suddenly started madly throwing things about.

I was impressed. Even Norman stopped cuddling the vacuum for a second to watch. She was marching about the room almost trashing it.

Anything she could lay her hands on was getting the full Mum throw-around.

'Weeeeeee!'

she cried, throwing cushions skywards. 'Like I said, anyone can do it.'

'Not bad for a beginner,' said Fiend. He may have his faults, but he could certainly give credit where credit was due.

Mum swept the table clean with one brush of her arm. 'How am I doing now?'

Haggis, Norman and Fiend held up scorecards.

'Only nine?' Mum was shocked.

'Yeah,' explained Fiend. 'There's no food on the ceiling. That's the sign of an amateur.'

'Silly me. Why didn't I think of that?'

Mum grabbed a carton of eggs out of the fridge and tossed one up to the ceiling. The yolk dripped down on her head. The monsters held up scorecards once again.

Ten this time.

'The room looks great. I love what you've done with the place.' Fiend really was impressed.

Everyone laughed. Mum laughed. I laughed. The monsters chuckled. Haggis laughed so much he let one go. Mum laughed some more. We were all having a great time laughing and pointing at the mess, and having fun and completely forgetting about the issue of the cleaning lady, when Mum suddenly stopped.

'Now *you* can clean it up.' Mum's face had gone right back to the angry look she had had on earlier. 'Every day I clean up after you. Now *you* can clean up after *me*.'

The monsters were horrified.

'You can't make us do this!' cried Fiend. 'It, it, it . . . it's **Unmonsterly!**'

Mum clearly didn't care. I don't know what yours is like, but I find there's only so far you can push a mother before she cracks. Mine was way past that line.

'Do it or you can find somewhere else to live. And stop hugging the vacuum cleaner, Norman. You have

WORK to do.'

And with that, she was gone.
I looked at the monsters. It was time
to act.

Soap and Water

'OK, listen up. Here are some cleaning products. These are rubber gloves.'

Fiend put one on his head.

'No. You wear them on your hands,' I said patiently.

'And they are not cow's udders and you don't milk them.' Haggis didn't get it either.

'And this is a feather duster. You use it for brushing away cobwebs.' I was really starting to think this might take a while. There was a sudden splash. I was right.

'No, that's a bucket,' I explained as calmly as I could. 'You fill it with

water and mop the floor.
The pool is now officially
closed.'

'Boring!'
said Fiend,
climbing out and
shaking the drops
off.

I ignored
him. 'Right,
I'll make a
start next door and you tidy
in here. Any questions?'

'When do we get a break?' said
Fiend.

'You don't. When Mum gets back,
she'll expect this house to be spotless.
So clean **EVERYTHING**.'

Now it was my turn to get wet. Haggis was attacking my head with a sponge. **'Not me Haggis!'** Angela wandered in just as Haggis tried cleaning a vase with his particularly bushy eyebrow.

'Wow, Haggis, I'm impressed,' she said.

'Well, thank you.' Haggis seemed genuinely touched.

'If Mum throws you out, I'll miss you, but I'll get over it. It could take

one second or it could take as many
as two.'

'Oh. You're making me blush,'
he said, kicking his foot shyly along
the carpet.

'OK, well, I'm going back to
my room now. So . . . let's do what
we usually do, shall we? You say
something really stupid and I'll try to
ignore it.' Angela waited a second.

'Would you like some banana peel?'
offered Haggis.

She was right. I **hate it** when
that happens.

There was no time to give it a second
thought, though. I grabbed a plastic
bag and started shovelling rubbish in.
There was work to be done, but only

by me it seemed. After a while, I felt an apple hit my shoulder, then a pear and, finally, a block of cheese.

'What's going on guys?'

'It's OK, human Eddie. We're really getting the hang of this tidying business.'

I turned and looked. Haggis was standing in the door of the fridge, throwing things out over his shoulder. Fiend was sitting on the sofa eating crisps.

'Haggis! What are you doing?'

'Ooh, fridge ready for inspection, sir!'

'YOU EMPTIED IT ALL OUT!'

'Yes, sir, thank you, sir,' agreed Haggis. 'Actually, it's frosty work. Fortunately, I have a fur coat.

Otherwise, I'd have got a chill.'

I turned to Fiend as he shovelled a handful of crisps into his mouth.

'And what are *you* doing?'

'I'm tidying these crisps away. Watch. I pick up the crisp. I put the crisp in my mouth. *Om.* I chew the crisp. I swallow the crisp.'

He did a big gulp. 'Ah, the crisp

is gone.'

'That's not tidying,' I argued. 'It's eating!'

'Wrong! There is no pleasure involved here. It's strictly business.'

I tried to reason with him. 'You're really not helping.'

He wasn't impressed with my attitude. 'My little green belly is fit to **burst** and that's all the thanks I get? Ha!' Fiend was the worst of the three of them for taking offence. I could tell because he wouldn't even look at me right now.

I was about to plead with

him and try to get him to see sense, but just then, I spotted Norman out of the corner of my eye. He had plucked a rose from the vase on the dining room table, popped it between his teeth and was now doing a tango with the vacuum cleaner.

'Why don't you do some cleaning with your girlfriend rather than just dancing about with her, Norman?' I was determined not to give up on any of them.

He stopped and looked at me with hurt in his eyes. I breathed deeply and counted to ten. Something my mum does when the monsters are being particularly frustrating.

'flob, wing, dicket, wibble.'

'Norman says he can't ask her
to clean the house on a first date.'
explained Fiend.

'Then I'll ask her.'
'Gleek, gumbo.'

'Norman wants you all to know
that if anyone looks at her, there'll
be **TROUBLE!**'

'Sprang, doo, weep, chik.'

'He says she's mine I tell you! All
mine! Get your own girlfriend.'

I sighed. Why did everything have
to be such hard work? I bet even being
the Prime Minister isn't even that much
of a stressful job, compared to trying
to keep my monsters in line when
they're being especially bonkers.

'You three are HOPELESS.'
I told them.

'Whoa! High praise!' Fiend was fanning himself with his hand. He really did think it was a compliment.

'That means a lot coming from you, Eddie.' Clearly, so did Haggis.

'You don't get it, do you?' I pleaded. 'When Dad tells you to do something, you can ignore it. When Mum tells you to do something, it's the **law**. If she gets back and this isn't finished, you'll be looking for somewhere else to live. Do you understand? She will chuck you out forever!'

'But cleaning is boring!' cried Haggis.

They just weren't getting it. It was time to try something else.

'Well, maybe cleaning doesn't have to be boring. Let's turn the radio on. Try to make it fun.'

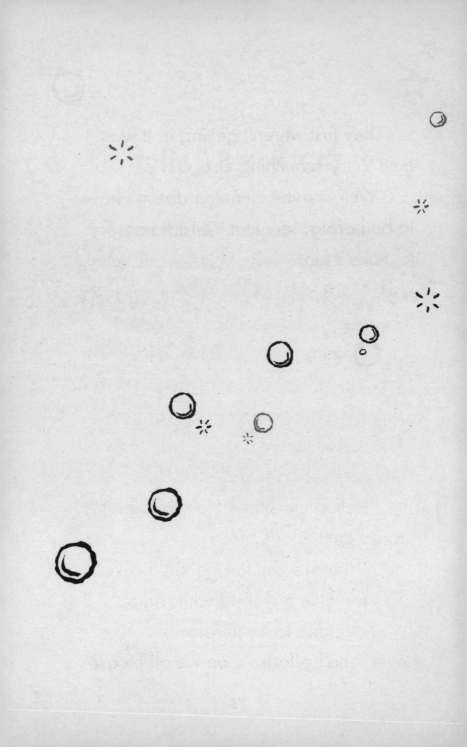

Our Next Caller

'It's eighteen degrees Celsius in the city on this beautiful, blue-skied, sunny afternoon.' The DJ was in full flow.

Haggis was staring, fascinated, at the radio. It would have been better all round if he had been dusting or polishing or something, but for now it looked like gazing at the radio was all we were going to get.

'Hello, little man.' He prodded the radio gently.

'Who are you talking to?' I asked.

'The little guy inside the radio.'

I decided to try to refocus everyone's efforts. 'Can we all please concentrate? Remember what Mum said.'

Fiend yawned and stretched out on the sofa. 'Right, here's the plan. Norman: rubbish duty. Haggis: wash up. Eddie: clean,' he said slowly, picking out a crisp from in-between his teeth.

'And what are you going to do?' I was curious to know, seeing as he was now stretching out for what looked to all the world like a sleep.

'I'm the boss. I'm going to watch you, and from time to time offer constructive criticism.' He shut one eye gently and adjusted a cushion as his pillow.

'People think it's easy. It's not, you know. Workers get blisters on their

hands; I get blisters on my *brain*.
Which would you prefer?'

I was keen to take this discussion
further, but I was distracted. Haggis
was now feeding cheese to the radio.

'Snack time, little man,' he said.

For a second, I very nearly felt what it must be like for Mum or Dad dealing with these three. 'You do know there's no one actually in there,' I said, trying to fish a small lump of Cheddar cheese out of the off switch.

'Then who's that speaking then?'

'It's a DJ – a disc jockey.'

'A jockey? Is his horse in there, too?'

I sighed and looked around, wondering if this place was ever going to be clean again. Not the way Haggis was currently doing things. He had stopped feeding the radio and was now licking plates with his enormous tongue. It was like watching a whale finishing off its dinner.

'Haggis!'

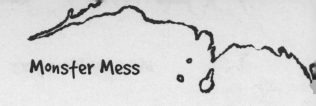

'Don't worry Eddie. After I tongue-
wash them, I give them a bit of a
bum-wipe.'

YUCK!

The plates were now wet and
sticky with red fur. I could just imagine
what my mum would think when she
saw them. In fact, I didn't even need
to imagine it. I knew exactly what
she would say, after that time Haggis
decided to help with the laundry and,
well, let's just say there was bottom fur
involved then and Mum had to throw
away her best work clothes.

'Very classy,' I said.

'The little man's
helping me. Aren't you,
tiny fellow?' Haggis
peered hopefully into the radio
and waved.

'Have you actually seen him?'
I didn't want to spoil his fun, but I
really was keen to get back to the
cleaning.

'No. He's . . . he's very shy. Doesn't
get out much.'

Suddenly, the song playing came
to an end and the DJ was talking once
again. Haggis smiled, as if hearing
from a long-lost friend.

'Hey, let's go to the phones. We
want to hear from you, the listener, so

call us on zero nine zero nine eight seven nine zero eight seven nine.'

Haggis stroked the radio gently.

'Don't you worry, little man. We all know you're in there.' With that, he turned, glared at me and marched out.

I felt bad, but I didn't have time to go after him. We were running out of time.

'Can we all **PLEASE** just get back to the cleaning?'

'I think you'll find it's my job to say that,' Fiend muttered crossly.

How come I was managing to upset everyone when none of this was actually *my* fault?

Suddenly Angela marched back into the kitchen. Oh great, this was all I needed.

'I'm bored, bored, bored. BORED!'

she announced. OK, Angela was clearly upset, too, but at least it wasn't my fault.

She kicked a piece of cheese across the floor as if to make sure we really got the message.

'I'M BORED!'

'I'm glad you're here,' said
Fiend. 'There's a monster emergency
happening and I'm in charge.'

Angela looked at him and snorted.
To anyone else that snort would have
been quite terrifying, but Fiend just
yawned. It would take a lot more than
an Angela snort to get him worried. In
fact, I think if Mum, Angela, a lion, a
tiger and a crazed rhino were in the
room right now, and all of them were
snorting, he would just wave his hand
about casually and demand a biscuit.
As it was, he was pointing at things he
wanted Angela to do.

'We need you to clean!'

'Oh, I'd love to help, yeah,
sincerely . . .' said Angela rolling her

eyes. 'Oh, wait, but I can't because I'm crazy busy right now talking to all my friends. Oh, hang on a minute. I haven't got any because they're all halfway across the world.'

'SSSSSHHH!'

I held my hand up. Someone was talking on the radio and I was fairly sure I recognized the voice. If not, it was someone doing a very good impression.

'OK, we have our first caller. You're through to Smile FM.' We all turned and looked at the radio.

'I'm Haggis,' said the caller.

I was right. That would be *our*

Haggis. One of the three creatures
on the planet I was supposed to be
keeping contained in the basement and
right now, not only was he nowhere
near the basement, he was talking to
the world at large.

'Haggis?'

Angela was moving towards the radio, just as surprised as I was to find him chatting away to the DJ and the listening public when, a few minutes ago, he'd been standing right in front of us, trying to secretly waft a smell away.

'What do you do, Haggis?' asked the DJ.

'I'm a monster.'

'Wait. I think I know this guy,' said Fiend, scratching his head. 'Is it Mr Prentice who lives down the road?'

'A monster? That sounds interesting.' The DJ was keen to find out more about his mystery caller.

And he was right. It could be really interesting, but not in a good

way. If Haggis suddenly
managed to broadcast
our secret to the whole
world, this would be very
bothersome indeed.

RING! RING!

Isn't That . . .?

'We're all monsters at heart, Haggis,' said the DJ. 'So . . . what's on your mind?'

I held my breath. This really was the last thing I needed right now.

'I'm having an argument with my friend Eddie.' Great. Haggis was clearly keen to get everything off his chest, paying special attention to my part in the proceedings.

'We don't have TIME for this!'

I shouted to no one in particular.

Haggis continued.
'Are you the little man
who lives in my radio?'

'Well, I guess I am,
yeah,' laughed the DJ. 'I'm the little
man who lives in your radio.'

'I knew it!' said Haggis. 'Did you
like the cheese?'

Just then the phone rang. I didn't
want to answer it, but I knew if I didn't,
it would just keep ringing. It was a call
I was dreading. Mum. To be fair, she
sounded quite calm; more in shock
than anything. She sounded like she'd
gone into that state she sometimes goes
in to, when everything has just got too
much for her in a dealing-with-monsters
sort of way. She goes very quiet and

gets a kind of crazy look in her eyes.
I imagine that Maria the cleaning lady
had a similar look on her face when
she ran away from our house.

'Hi, Mum. Yeah, we're listening.
I know . . .'

I missed the next bit of the
conversation, but from what little I
could gather, the DJ and Haggis were
still getting along like a house on fire.

'OK, we're on the phone with
Haggis. So, tell us, Haggis, what's
happening with you?'

'I'm in trouble, little man. Big time.
The house is a mess and human mum
thingy person has asked us to clean
it up!'

I heard my mum make a sort of
a squeaking noise so I gently put the
phone down. I thought it best if I heard
everything that was being said right
now, just in case I had to give evidence
at my own trial in the Court of Mum
and Dad. From what I could gather,
the DJ was a little confused. Not that
I could blame him.

'Human mum thingy person?' he
asked.

To be fair to Haggis, he was keen
to explain everything fully.

'Yeah! Do you know her? Yeah,
yeah . . . anyway, anyway, she went
completely COCONUTS!'

'Do you mean bananas?' The DJ
was still desperate to have all the

facts and I suppose, eventually, get
to the bottom of the matter. Haggis,
meanwhile, was doing his best to give
answers by chuntering on.

'Oh, yeah – them, too. Did I tell you
I've got horns?'

Just then Angela's mobile
rang. She shot me a look
before answering it.
'Hi, Dad . . . yeah. We know.
Great, isn't it?'

'Sssshhh,' said Fiend. 'This is
brilliant. This guy really does sound like
someone we know. If I could
just put my finger on who
it might be.'

'Is there anything
else you'd like to get

off your chest, Haggis?' The DJ
was still grilling him.

'Well, my friend
Norman's in love with
a vacuum cleaner, but
don't tell anyone. No,
it's early days. All very hush-hush.'

'He's in love with a
vacuum cleaner?'

I held my head in my hands.
I would have tried to stop Haggis from
carrying on, but there was never any
point. It was a bit like trying to push
a lorry up a hill: a lot of effort, but no
chance of you ever achieving your
goal, with quite a strong possibility
that you might just end up flat on
your face.

'Is this some kind of an on-off relationship?' The DJ laughed at his own rubbish joke. I decided I didn't like him much.

'Swarfle,' said Norman, holding the vacuum cleaner tightly to him.

'No, it's real,' continued Haggis. 'It's like that film with that guy and the girl and the guy really likes the girl and she really likes him, but then they eat each other or something.'

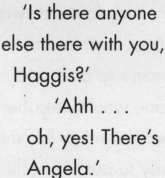

'Is there anyone else there with you, Haggis?'

'Ahh . . . oh, yes! There's Angela.'

We all turned and looked at her. She was turning the colour of my gym socks.

Haggis was pushing on, making sure there could be absolutely no misunderstanding of who he was talking about this time.

'Angela Carlson.

C-A-R-L-S-O-N

of Hill Gate High School.'

Angela sat down heavily. I was about to point out to her that maybe it wasn't so bad. Maybe this new-found fame would help her get to know people. I was just thinking of the best way to put my point across when I realized that Haggis hadn't finished.

'Now I know she says she's got no friends, but we all like her because she's **smelly** like us.'

'Oh, no,' said Angela. '*No, no, no, no, no*. Please tell me this isn't happening.'

'OK, a big stinky hi to Angela Carlson!' cheered the DJ.

I'm afraid it was. That red-sock colour on her face went even brighter.

'Phew, he has got a point,' said Fiend, wafting the air with his hands.

Angela leapt to her feet again. 'I don't smell!'

'Yeah, you do.' Fiend pulled a face.

'Phheeewwweee!'

'It's called *soap!*' cried Angela.

'Get off the phone, Haggis.' I yelled as loudly as I could. 'We're busy! We don't have time for this!'

Haggis must have heard me. There was now a sort of shuffling noise going on upstairs.

'I've got to go now, little man,' he continued on the radio.

'Nice talking to you, Haggis,' said the DJ. 'It's been a lot of fun.'

'Bye.'

The DJ started playing a song.
We all sat in stunned silence for a
second before Haggis wandered in
cheerfully.

'I've got it,' cried Fiend. 'It was
you!' He pointed at Haggis. 'You were
in the *radio!*'

'Doo doo doo doo doo!'

sang Norman, cuddling the vacuum
cleaner, still very much a monster
in love.

'I was?' Haggis said, scratching
his nose.

'Yeah! We heard you. You were
talking drivel!'

'That *was* me!' cheered Haggis.

'I always talk drivel!'

I lost it completely.

'Can't you see? This is going to land us in even more trouble!' I cried. 'And we still haven't actually done any **CLEANING**!'

One Unhappy Sister

'Congratulations, Haggis. I am now officially in the social wilderness.' Angela was sitting on the floor rocking backwards and forwards unhappily.

'Did you hear me then?' Haggis was basking in all the attention. If we weren't careful, this could all go to his head.

'Oh, yeah,' said Angela.

'And so did the human mum thingy person. In fact, if I know her well, which I think I do, she'll be rushing home right now to congratulate you in person. Yeah, so keep in touch. Don't be strangers. We'll be text buddies.'

'**Brr brr. Brr brr. Brr!**' Norman was now down on one knee, singing some sort of Norman-like love song to the vacuum cleaner. To my untrained ear it sounded more like someone trying to start a particularly old lawn mower, but then again, I'm not a monster so maybe I was missing out on something quite beautiful. Angela ignored this moment of love completely and snorted loudly once again.

It was becoming a habit with her.
'It's not as though I'll ever have
anyone else to talk to anyway.'

She stormed out, slamming the door
behind her, something she's getting
good at. Before she went, though, she
grabbed a can of air-freshener and
quickly sprayed it around herself. She
really had taken to heart the monsters'
comment about being smelly.

'That's it,' I said. I sank into a chair
completely deflated. 'We're **finished**.'
'If Mum's on her way home, we are
officially done.'

'We are? Great!' cheered Fiend.
'I'm exhausted.' He rolled over on the
sofa and shut his eyes. Quite what he
had to be tired about I'll never know,

seeing as he hadn't actually done
anything.

'Don't you lot get it?' I pleaded. 'It's
all over!'

'Yes, and the sense of satisfaction
is enormous!' cheered Fiend. 'And you
thought we couldn't manage it.'

The DJ suddenly piped up again.
'Just to let you know, folks, the last few
minutes we've been inundated with texts
and emails wishing Haggis and the
crew good luck with the clean-up,
so this next track is for Haggis
and all you monsters out there
as you work.'

Fiend sat bolt upright.
'Hey! That's us! We're
FAMOUS!'

Before I had time to gasp with
shock, he was up and dancing about
to the music, feather duster in hand,
actually doing some cleaning. That's
the thing with monsters, as I'm sure
I've already mentioned. Completely
unpredictable. Then, before I could
blink, Haggis had joined in too.

'That's it, guys! Tidy everything
you see,' I cheered them on. Well,
you have to seize the moment with a
monster, as I'm sure you know. If you
waste a golden opportunity like this,
when they are actually doing what they
should be, it can be weeks before you
get another chance.

Haggis took me at my word, picked up Fiend and threw him away.

'AHHH! NOT ME!'

Even Norman was joining in. In front of my very eyes, rubbish was being cleared, dust was being dusted, surfaces were being polished and the floor was once again reappearing from underneath the mountain of filth. It almost looked like our house as we used to know it.

Well, It Looks Familiar

Mum and Dad walked in and looked around. Even though I say so myself, the place was spotless. You could have eaten your dinner off the floor. I know that for a fact because Fiend actually did and, to be fair to him, he immediately cleaned it up afterwards. It was almost like their moment of fame on the radio had turned them all into Olympic cleaning medal-winners.

'Don't get your hopes up. We've obviously walked into the wrong house.' Dad was wandering about now, touching things that looked familiar.

'It *looks* like our house,' Mum said, running a finger along the surfaces, looking for dust.

Not that she would have found any; Haggis and Norman had seen to that. Well, Haggis had eaten most of it, but at least it was gone. Just then, Angela wandered back in, still in a sulk and looking for someone to take the blame for her bad mood. She almost gasped when she saw how clean everything was.

'Whoa! Photo opportunity, although you know I probably would've preferred a photo of the monsters leaving, but hey.'

Mum eyed her suspiciously. 'That *sounds* like our daughter.'

Dad poked Angela in the face,

checking her over to make sure.

'Could be a lookalike. I'm taking no chances. Something very strange has happened to our house and whatever it was that made it look like this might have affected our children, as well.'

Fiend, Haggis and Norman burst into song.

'I've been working like a monster . . .' Fiend warbled.

'But we ain't done yet,' Haggis joined in behind him.

'Noop, doo, noop, noop, noop, waaahhh.'

Norman finished it all off in his best falsetto.

'My handy helpers, *you did it*!
The place looks **fabulous**.' Mum was
almost overcome with emotion.

Fiend leaned back against the
table, casually picking his teeth with
a front-door key.

'Yeah, well, you know. Some say
it's all just a case of hard work and
dedication.'

'Are you sure you didn't just hire someone else to clean?' Dad still had his suspicions. Not that you could blame him. He might be a dad, but even they can be clever sometimes.

'So you won't chuck them out then?' I thought it best to take advantage of Mum and Dad feeling in a particularly good mood towards the monsters.

They thought about it for a second.

'I suppose it would be quite mean to throw them out after they did such a good job in here.'

The monsters and I smiled and hugged each other. This was the best news we had heard so far today.

'In fact, as they did such a great job, they can clean *every* week!'

Mum was looking smug even as she spoke. That was the worst news *ever*. Didn't she know how much hard work for me that would be?

'OH! BUT...'

shouted Haggis and Fiend together, suddenly almost speechless for once. I suppose there has to be good and bad in everything.

'What's the matter, Norman? Have you got girlfriend trouble?' He was staring at the floor sadly and sniffing every now and then.

'Boop, weee, dwacko.'

'Apparently, she fancies the little man in the radio now.' Fiend was back into full translation mode.

'Doo doo, doo doo, doo doo.'

'Norman says he thought it was true love. Apparently not.'

'Ding!' Norman sniffed even more loudly.

'Norman says he has news for this heartbreaker.'

Dad was looking completely lost. It was Angela's turn to be the interpreter.

'It's simple really. Norman's been dumped by the vacuum cleaner.'

That was all too much for the little furry fellow. With that, he burst into full-blown tears and hurled himself on to the floor, banging the carpet with his fists. A bit like I used to when I was a toddler and Angela stood on my toys. If you don't believe me, watch the video Dad made. The one he shows every time he really wants to embarrass me.

'I think perhaps
it's best if we leave
him to it,' said
Fiend, heading
back towards the
basement. I sighed to myself and
shook my head. If he'd headed back
to the basement this morning when I
told him to, and left Maria to clean the
house, it might saved us a lot of effort
(and saved Angela from quite a lot of
embarrassment). But there you go, that's
monsters for you.

Fiend stopped and looked back at
Norman. 'He'll get over it soon enough.
He'd completely forgotten about the
microwave five minutes after she
dumped him. Then it was all we could

do to stop him banging on
about the coffee-maker.'

We all nodded and
followed him, leaving
Norman gently
whimpering into his
armpits. And Fiend
was right. Two seconds
later, Norman stopped suddenly and
ran off to cuddle the telly. I smiled at
Fiend and Haggis. Sweet really, when
you think about it, especially as we
had nearly got ourselves into huge
trouble with Maria, Haggis on the
radio and then the cleaning issues.

We'd learnt an important lesson
today. When Mum tells you to do
something, you have to do it.

But it doesn't pay to do it too well.

Me & My MONSTERS™

for more monster mayhem

www.meandmymonsters.co.uk

or

www.meandmymonsters.com.au

Meet the Monsters

FIEND

Noisy! Never stops talking

full of (bad) ideas and advice

Boss of the monsters – because he says so!

NORMAN

Big sticky-out nose

Makes weird noises that's just how he speaks

He's not crazy he just seems that way.

HAGGIS

Whopping monster body

Scares very easily

Eats everything - you might just hear his belly ringing one day.

It all started with a Scarecrow.

Puffin is seventy years old.
Sounds ancient, doesn't it? But Puffin has never been
so lively. We're always on the lookout for the next big
idea, which is how it began all those years ago.

Penguin Books was a big idea from the mind of
a man called Allen Lane, who in 1935 invented
the quality paperback and changed the world.
**And from great Penguins, great Puffins grew,
changing the face of children's books forever.**

The first four Puffin Picture Books were hatched in 1940 and the
first Puffin story book featured a man with broomstick arms called
Worzel Gummidge. In 1967 Kaye Webb, Puffin Editor, started the
Puffin Club, promising to **'make children into readers'**.
She kept that promise and over 200,000 children became
devoted Puffineers through their quarterly instalments of
Puffin Post, which is now back for a new generation.

Many years from now, we hope you'll look back and
remember Puffin with a smile. **No matter what your age
or what you're into, there's a Puffin for everyone.**
The possibilities are endless, but one thing is for sure:
whether it's a picture book or a paperback, a sticker book
or a hardback, **if it's got that little Puffin
on it – it's bound to be good.**